Parents and Caregivers

Stone Arch Readers are designed to provide enjoyable reading experiences, as well as opportunities to develop vocabulary, literacy skills, and comprehension. Here are a few ways to support your beginning reader:

- Talk with your child about the ideas addressed in the story.

- Discuss each illustration, mentioning the characters, where they are, and what they are doing.

- Read with expression, pointing to each word. You may want to read the whole story through and then revisit parts of the story to ensure that the meanings of words or phrases are understood.

- Talk about why the character did what he or she did and what your child would do in that situation.

- Help your child connect with characters and events in the story.

Remember, reading with your child should be fun, not forced. Each moment spent reading with your child is a priceless investment in his or her literacy life.

Gail Saunders-Smith, Ph.D.

STONE ARCH **READERS**

are published by Stone Arch Books
A Capstone Imprint
151 Good Counsel Drive, P.O. Box 669
Mankato, Minnesota 56002
www.capstonepub.com

Library of Congress Cataloging-in-Publication Data
Suen, Anastasia.
Test drive : a Robot and Rico story / by Anastasia Suen ; illustrated by Mike Laughead.
p. cm. — (Stone Arch readers)
ISBN 978-1-4342-1868-1 (library binding)
ISBN 978-1-4342-2303-6 (pbk.)
[1. Automobiles, Racing—Fiction. 2. Toys—Fiction. 3. Robots—Fiction.] I. Laughead, Mike, ill.
II. Title. PZ7.S94343Te 2010
[E]—dc22
2009034211

Summary: Robot builds a race car, and Rico wants to drive it. However, the car has lots of
problems and doesn't work properly.

Art Director: Bob Lentz
Graphic Designer: Hilary Wacholz

Reading Consultants:
Gail Saunders-Smith, Ph.D.
Melinda Melton Crow, M.Ed.
Laurie K. Holland, Media Specialist

TEST DRIVE

BY ANASTASIA SUEN
ILLUSTRATED BY MIKE LAUGHEAD

A
ROBOT
AND
RICO
STORY

STONE ARCH BOOKS
a capstone imprint

This is **ROBOT**.
Robot has lots of tools.

He uses the tools to help his
best friend, **Rico**.

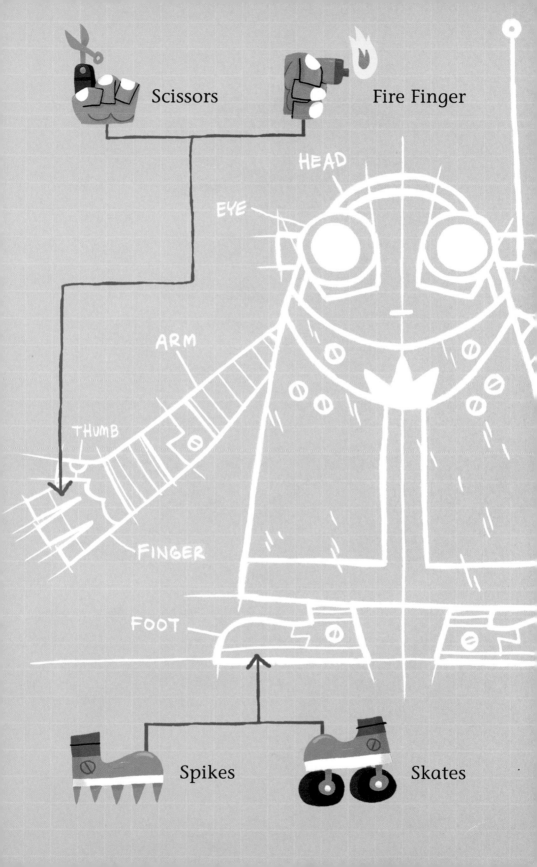

Scissors

Fire Finger

HEAD

EYE

ARM

THUMB

FINGER

FOOT

Spikes

Skates

Robot is busy at his workbench.

"What are you doing?" asks Rico.

"I'm building a race car,"
says Robot.

"I know how to drive," says Rico.

"I have to test it first," says Robot.

"Okay," says Rico. "But then it's my turn."

Robot puts the car on the ground.

The car goes forward. The car goes backward.

"Is it my turn yet?" asks Rico.

"I have to test it on the track first," says Robot.

"What track?" asks Rico.

"Follow me," says Robot.

Robot puts the car on the track.

"Wow! Is it my turn yet?"
asks Rico.

"I have to test it first," says Robot.

"Okay," says Rico. "But then it's my turn."

The car goes down the track and crashes.

"The wheels aren't working," says Robot.

Robot picks up the car and turns it over. He moves the stick. The wheels turn.

"It works now," says Robot.

"Is it my turn yet?" asks Rico.

"I have to test it again first,"
says Robot.

"Okay," says Rico. "But then
it's my turn."

Robot puts the car back on the track. He moves the stick.

The car goes down the track. It crashes again.

"Oh no," says Robot.

"Not again," says Rico.

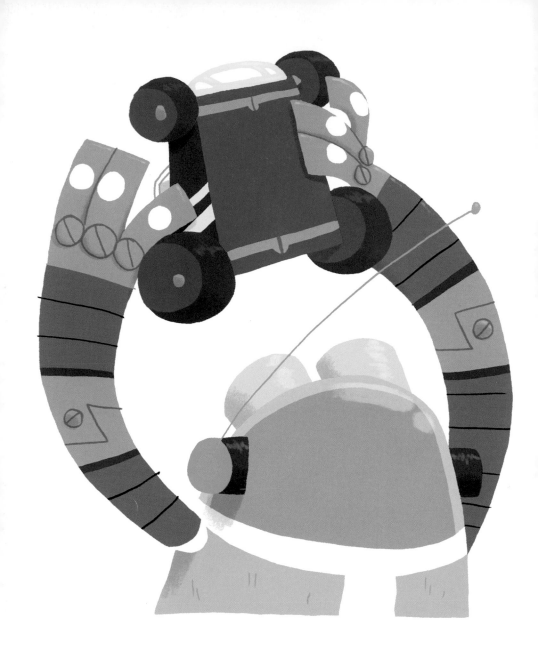

Robot picks up the car.

"Let's try it here instead," he says.

He puts the car on the ramp.
It still doesn't work.

"Forget the car," says Robot.

"Why? I didn't get to drive!"
says Rico.

"I have a better idea,"
says Robot.

Robot throws Rico the control.

"It's finally your turn," says Robot.

"What do you mean?" asks Rico.

When he pushes a button, Robot turns into a race car.

"Cool!" says Rico.

"You are a good driver,"
says Robot.

"I just needed to wait for my turn," says Rico.

STORY WORDS

workbench forward track

drive backward wheels

Total Word Count: 311

One robot. One boy. One crazy fun friendship! Read all the Robot and Rico adventures!

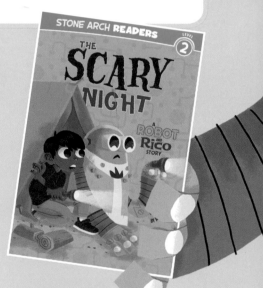